No Good Deed

by Lisa M. Lane

A Rosie McMahon SoCal Mystery

Grousable Books

This is a short story by Lisa M. Lane. It was first published in *A Warm Mug of Cozy Anthology*, Volume 2, 2024.

More information on her other books can be found at https://grousablebooks.com.

This is a work of fiction. Any resemblance of characters to any actual person, living or dead, is purely coincidental.

Published by Grousable Books
Encinitas, California
ISBN 979-8-9890337-8-2

No Good Deed

"I don't see a story here," whispered Lou as Rosie continued to pick the lock on the garage. It wasn't terribly late, only about ten, but it was dark in the alley. Lou tried not to block the dim light from the neighbor's house and looked around for interlopers. Then it occurred to him that *they* were the interlopers.

"You will get your story once I get into this beast." At seventy-three years old, Rosie was still spry enough to crouch down and do the job. Not that picking locks was her thing; she much preferred problems that could be solved with calculated thinking and some computerized instruments. But now and then . . .

Click!

"We're in," she whispered to Lou. Together they slowly lifted the garage door, but stopped when it squeaked. Rosie whipped out a can of 3-in-1 oil, dripped some onto the brackets, and handed it to Lou. He popped the red top closed and put it in his pocket. Then he hitched up his pants. How could he have been expected to remember a belt with all this going on?

They had assumed the garage would be full of junk, stuff piled to the ceiling. It wasn't. Everything was stacked neatly around the edges of the room, up to the rafters and the sill of the frosted window. But in the middle of the garage was a red leather chair, and in the chair slouched the body of a man. He was wearing a Dodgers cap.

Lou gasped, struggling to keep his voice down.

"You didn't say anything about a body!" he hissed.

"I didn't know!" she hissed back.

This complicated matters considerably. The clues had led Rosie, amateur sleuth and acknowledged busybody of San Benno, to this garage. She was looking for a packet or envelope containing an old property deed. The owner of the garage was out of town; she had made sure of that. So who was in the red leather chair?

Lou blew out the breath he'd been holding and listened. There was no sound. The alley behind Fourth Street was silent. Dead silent, Lou thought. Damn, he was already writing the story for the San Benno Bugle in his head. Because now there was definitely a story.

"We should get out of here," he said, trying

to be practical.

"Don't be ridiculous," Rosie murmured as she kneeled before the body. "I don't see any wound. No bullet hole or blood."

"Don't touch anything! I'm calling the police."

"Just doing a bit of looking," said Rosie, pulling a pen out of her pocket and carefully lifting the victim's arm by the sleeve. "I need a light."

Torn between dialing 911 and lending a hand, Lou looked around for a switch. Shaking his head at his own stupidity, he instead got out his cell phone and clicked the flashlight app, carefully shining the beam where Rosie was looking.

She tipped up the Dodgers cap. Just a gray face, eyes closed. Rosie took out a tissue and used it to pry open an eyelid. Lou shined the light and saw little red dots on the whites. His stomach turned just a bit. He may have been tough, but she had been a nurse in Vietnam. Rosie waved down toward the man's neck. The red mark was obvious.

"Strangled or hanged," she said.

"I'm sure the coroner could tell you that. May I call the police now?"

She was sitting back on her heels, peering up at the dead man's face. It had a few days' growth of black beard speckled with gray. "Does he look familiar to you?"

"Vaguely. May I call the police now?"

Rosie stood and considered.

"He's been here awhile. How long has Ron Voss been away?"

"Almost two weeks. May I call the police now?"

"Oh, sure. We'll say we're here because...?"

"We heard a sound?" That was foolish. They'd picked the lock, although they didn't have to admit to that. They came along and the garage door was open? The neighbors would know it hadn't been. Lou sighed. He knew when Rosie called him that this hadn't been a good idea, but now it was a very, very bad idea.

"Anonymous tip," he said, nodding decisively.

Rosie was looking at the shelves now.

"On a cell phone?" she said, taking down an Oxford box marked "Papers" in Sharpie. Lou had to admire the way she was using the tissue to avoid fingerprints. He decided helping was the fastest way to get them out of there, so he shone the light on the box as Rosie flipped through the files.

"Aha!" she said, pulling out a manila folder that said "Deeds". It was almost an inch thick. She removed it and replaced the lid. Lou returned the box to the shelf.

Suddenly there was a crash out in the alley,

like something metal falling. They froze.

"What was that?" whispered Lou. Her hearing had been better than his for some time.

She crept to the open door and peered around the corner, then exhaled in relief.

"Raccoon. Knocked over the trash can."

They gently closed the garage door as they stepped into the alley. Rosie picked up the lock and waved for Lou to shine the phone.

"This will re-lock, but Rory will know it's been picked." Rory Gallardo was the police detective, the only one in San Benno. The beach town could have used more, but his capable sergeants took up much of the slack.

She locked the garage and the two of them walked very quietly until they got to her house. Hephaestus meowed from his spot on the railing, making Lou jump.

"Hush, Hephaestus," said Rosie as she unlocked the front door. "You'll give Lou a heart attack."

Lou huffed and followed the cat into the house. "He won't give me a heart attack. Why do you always think I'm going to have a heart attack?"

Rosie put the kettle on in the kitchen. Lou was just grumpy because he'd been scared. Or because Lou was just grumpy.

He plopped into his usual chair at the table, and Hephaestus jumped into his lap.

"May I call the police now, woman?"

"How about in the morning?" Rosie said, holding out a box of Japanese green tea and a box of Rooibos. Lou pointed to the Rooibos and grumbled something about there never being any coffee.

"Because," she continued, "the body's clearly been there awhile, and the garage is all locked up again. We could go to the station and talk to Rory personally. Confess what we did."

Lou didn't like the way she'd been referring to Inspector Gallardo by his first name lately. He wasn't jealous. Rory Gallardo was decades younger and happily married to Amy. It rankled because despite his hints at greater togetherness, Rosie was quite content to be an independent widow. And a good friend. And a good hostess, he thought as she got a coffee cake out of the fridge and started slicing.

Rory Gallardo came to work at the San Benno Police Station in a good mood. The sun was out, a breeze was coming up from the ocean, and his wife Amy had a half day at work so she'd made him breakfast. What a great day, he thought, glad he no longer lived in L.A. and happy running his very own police station.

"Hello, Sergeant Robles!" he said cheerily as he breezed in the front door. But Jane Robles looked bemused rather than delighted to see him.

"Mrs. McMahon and Lou Kline are in your office, Detective."

Glancing over at the counter in dismay, he saw Hephaestus the orange tabby nonchalantly pushing papers onto the floor. The on-duty volunteer was smiling at the feline indulgently. It would not be a great day after all.

After the usual salutations, Rosie contritely explained about the friends she'd been asked to help, when it all went wrong.

"So you say these friends are members of the Koko Island Club?" Rory asked again, looking at what was becoming a full page of scribbled notes he wouldn't be able to decipher later.

"Yes. They don't own the island, of course.

But they take a boat over to gather once a month."

"And you are a member, Mrs. McMahon?" Lou was already shaking his head, but as a negative response or in despair Rory couldn't tell.

"Yes, but I only just joined last week. My friend Marcia suggested it. My online friend, that is. We haven't met up in a while, although we knew each other well serving in Vietnam."

Rory remembered vaguely about Rosie being a wartime nurse or something, which was supposed to help explain her alacrity with computers, although he'd never quite understood the connection himself. His notes were a mess. He went to the office door and asked Sergeant Robles to come in.

"Sergeant, do you know anything about this Koko Island Club?"

"Yes, sir, they've been meeting out on that

island for years. An overnight trip about once a month. Never any trouble. The department has a boat down at the Lifeguard station but we've never been called out there." She shrugged.

Rory turned back to the pair of senior miscreants, noticing that Lou was slouching lower in his seat. That couldn't be good. Newspaper reporters didn't hide.

"So they asked me to look into some paperwork about the island. I love research." Rosie smiled benignly.

"And did you discover something?"

Rosie hesitated. "Well, yes, in a manner of speaking. Some of the members of the club were talking about raising money to buy the big house out there. No one ever uses it, but it's locked up so the club can't use it either. They asked me to help find out who owned it. But I was unable to find the deed in the usual places."

Rory waited. He knew there'd be more. Lou cleared his throat and looked miserably out the window.

"Mr. Voss, though, is a lawyer. One of the members suggested that he might know who owned the place, but he'd asked and Voss had refused to divulge. It seemed like a dead end. Until Voss went on vacation."

He heard Jane's intake of breath. "You didn't," she said quietly.

"We did," Lou groaned. "Went by his house last night. Broke into the garage."

"I see." Rory wrote "breaking and entering" on his notepad.

"And found more than we bargained for," Lou grumbled, leaning forward in his chair now with his elbows on his knees. "The body of a man in a chair."

"He is wearing a Dodgers cap," Rosie added helpfully. "Looks like he's been there awhile.

Strangulation or hanging. A cold room so he doesn't smell too bad."

There was simply, absolutely no point in telling them they shouldn't be doing things like this. Rory could talk law, he could talk rules, he could make them promise never to do it again. He could call Mr. Voss and get them sued, call the sheriff, put them both behind bars, at least for a while. If they had bars. Right now all he had was the staff room. It was a small police station.

"Ohhhh—kay. Sergeant Robles, please take Sergeant Maura and get right over to the garage at . . . ?"

"The alley behind 842 Fourth Street," said Rosie cooperatively.

". . . the alley behind 842 Fourth Street. Take the good camera, and I'll call the medical examiner's office and tell them to send someone."

Duty done, Rosie rose to go. Lou hadn't moved. As much as Rory wanted to say something hostile, angry, and likely regrettable, he instead focused on Lou's profession.

"Mr. Kline, it should go without saying that we don't want any premature coverage in the press?"

Lou looked up, and an uncertain expression crossed his face. He opened his mouth, changed his mind, hung his head, and nodded.

"Good," said the detective. "I will visit both of you later for" — he stifled a sigh — "more details."

Rosie had put Hephaestus on his cat harness

for the walk home, and Lou was lagging behind.

"Rory was very nice, wasn't he?" said Rosie over her shoulder.

"Too nice. He should have arrested us right there. We were breaking and entering. And stealing." He looked pointedly at Rosie.

"I borrowed some papers. I'll put them back. But who do you think the man is? And who killed him?"

Lou stopped walking and Rosie had to turn to talk to him.

"Rosie-me-darling, I don't mind saying that at the moment I don't care. I am late for work, where editing a lousy story about the San Benno High School marching band awaits me." He gave an old-fashioned bow and began heading across the street.

"Work, work, work," piped Rosie. "You know where to find me!"

He did. In her garden shed slash office,

happily Googling to find out more about Koko Island and its history. Her love was research and goodness knows it could get her into trouble or, sometimes, out of it.

Two days later and we're on the trail, thought Rosie. Or rather the water. Poor Lou was looking a little green as the police boat crossed the channel to Koko Island. Rory was in his element, enjoying the sea breeze as Sergeant Diego Maura steered the craft. The four members of the Koko Island Club huddled together in the stern. Rosie knew them all now, at least a little. Mark Jacob, the astronomy teacher, had brought a telescope that took up about a third of the seating. Karen Aguilar, antiques dealer, was next to him, her bright orange hair blowing out from under her scarf. The brothers, Drew and Hoppy, sported Hawaiian shirts and had brought beer. Rory kept frowning at them. Last of the passengers was Arnold from the medical examiner's office, hoping to see some dolphins.

The boat was heavily loaded for an overnight trip, and the proximity of everyone to everyone else meant that secrets about the case weren't going to be kept. After the medical examiner had called last night with the autopsy report, word had gotten around that the man had not been killed at 842 Fourth Street at all, but possibly on the island. Once shown a photo, all four members of the club recognized him as the man they'd seen briefly on the island at their last meeting.

"He joined us to look through the telescope," Mark Jacob had said. "Said his name was Tom. Went off somewhere after that."

"We had no idea anyone but us went there," said Hoppy for the fourth time, as the boat skimmed on the glassy water. "We thought it was our place."

"Do you really think he died on the island?" Karen asked.

"Won't know till we get there," said Rory. He was still trying to figure out why Mrs. McMahon and Mr. Kline were on the trip at all. She had gotten the group together, it was true. But it was Arnold from the M.E.'s office, overjoyed at seeing her again for the first time since the war, who'd insisted she go along. Rory suspected that Arnold was why Lou was there, practically hanging over the side. Out of the corner of his eye, he saw Rosie slip some bands onto Lou's wrists.

"So did Mr. Voss know this guy at all?" Arnold eagerly asked Rosie.

"We don't know," said Rosie. "No one has

been able to reach Mr. Voss."

The channel was wide and for some time no one spoke. Lou was feeling better and was starting to doze off, as were the brothers. Rosie and Arnold were talking quietly, and the intrepid Miss Aguilar was trying to read a book. By the time they arrived at the island, all of them looked exhausted except Sergeant Diego Maura and Arnold. They jumped onto the dock, tied off the boat, and grabbed their gear.

"We need to stay here near the dock," explained Rory, helping everyone off. "Arnold and Sergeant Maura need to look around, but they plan to focus on the house. We can set up for the night here in the dock house."

The dock house was just a room in a large shed, but there was a sink and a toilet on a septic tank, and wood for the fireplace. Terrified of being bored, Miss Aguilar had brought a bag full of paperback books which she was happy to share. Rosie grabbed the John LeCarré, and Lou reached for Jared Diamond's *Collapse*. The twins had brought cards and dice, and set up a game with Mark Jacob, who kept interrupting with tidbits about odds and probabilities. Rory tried to text his wife Amy, but there was no signal.

"What are those things?" Rory asked Lou, pointing at the bands on his wrists. Lou shrugged.

"Sea bands," said Rosie. "They're brilliant for nausea."

The sun was setting by the time Arnold and Sergeant Maura returned from their explorations, both smiling.

"He was killed here, right behind the big house," said Diego.

Arnold nodded. "No question. I can't do the DNA here, but the rope matches the marks on the victim's neck and the soil there looks the same as what I found on his shoes."

Rory was less happy. "So we have a man, seen here, killed here. Your report"–he nodded to Arnold–"pegged the death at about two weeks ago".

"Maggots," interjected Rosie. Lou rolled his eyes.

"And two weeks ago," continued Rory, "was when you all had your last overnight."

It would be unkind to say that the members of the Koko Island Club weren't bright. Karen Aguilar read many books, Mark Jacob was a teacher, and the twins ran a car repair business. But somehow it hadn't occurred to any of them that they were under suspicion.

"I thought we were here to verify things and show you around," said Mark Jacob, swallowing.

"You are," said Rory, "and we have just about another hour of daylight for that. But I'm afraid that if you four were here, and the victim was here, the conclusion is pretty nasty."

It wasn't light yet, but Rosie was accustomed to getting up early. She was achy from sleeping on the cot in the dock house. The brothers had gone outside to sleep on the grassy hill, and Diego was in the boat, but everyone else had been inside.

"You're up early." It was Rory Gallardo, doing some stretches under a tree. He had built a small fire in an old clay fountain.

"Yes. I can't make tea or I'll wake everyone."

"I have coffee here," said Rory.

Rosie smiled. "Somehow I never imagined you as Mr. REI."

"Yeah. I used to be up in the mountains above L.A., on puma watch. Sometimes it would be cold, so I learned to do this. What's life without coffee?"

Rosie started imitating his stretches, trying to get the night out of her joints. "You know, I did some research on the club members before we left. And on who the victim might be."

Of course she had. Rory was chagrined that he had not, although he'd asked Sergeant Robles to follow up on who owned the island and the house. That had gone nowhere.

"What have we got?" he said in what he hoped was his best TV cop cooperation voice.

"My papers are inside, but Lou was able to help me get a list of some of Voss's clients. I was thinking that the location of the body might be designed to show a connection. And, you see, I have the deed."

Rory stopped stretching. "You do? How? When?"

"It was in Voss's records." She leaned

sideways, lifted her arm, and looked up at the brightening sky as if things were written there. "The owner of this island, and the house on it, is a Thomas Zinn. An astrophysicist. Made his money in aerospace, back before the big slump in the nineties."

This could be helpful, thought Rory. I can find out who knew him, and in what capacity, using his name. Rosie continued.

"I thought that our companions were avoiding saying much about the man they found here. It must be him. My question was whether any of them had a reason to do him harm. Strangulation, or hanging, seems like a rather personal form of killing."

There were stirrings from the dock house as the others awakened.

"Thank you, Mrs. McMahon."

"Rosie, please."

"Rosie. As we get toured around, I'll be

asking questions. I hope it's OK to say that I'd appreciate it if you didn't?" He congratulated himself on not telling her directly not to interfere.

She smiled. "I'll just be listening, Detective. Just listening."

Rory did notice that as the group walked up the hill, Rosie was always situated to hear him conversing with the club members.

"So, Mr. Jacob — "

"Doctor Jacob."

"Doctor Jacob. You said that the man on the island came to look through your telescope?"

"Yes. I usually bring it and the others like looking at things. It's like teaching without all the stress and exams." He took off his round glasses and wiped them with the tail of his shirt as he walked.

"And he said his name was Tom?" Mark Jacob nodded. "Did he say anything else?"

"Not really. Just 'nice telescope', I think." He looked thoughtful. "I did see something else that might interest you, though." He looked around. "Karen Aguilar said when I was setting up the telescope that she was going up to the porch of the big house to read a book. But when I went to find her, she wasn't there. I thought I saw her later talking to someone near the boat, but I assumed it was one of the brothers. Now I'm not so sure."

Karen Aguilar was not forthcoming.

"How do I know exactly when I might have talked to Drew or Hoppy? I don't have regular conversations with them, that's for sure. The only interest we share is this island. I could care less about cars, girls, and beer."

"Did you know who the new man on the island was?"

"Nope. I just know he was talking to Mark at the telescope."

"Did you see him at any other time?"

She shook her head. "No, but there is something you should know." She looked around, but the others were walking in pairs up the hill. "The brothers went out later that night. I woke up because I forgot to bring in my medicine case from the boat, and I noticed they weren't in the dock house. On my way back from the boat, I saw three people together at the bottom of the hill. The others were inside."

"You think they were talking to this Tom person?"

"Who else?"

When asked, the brothers admitted to talking to Tom in the wee hours.

"What were you talking about?"

Hoppy shook his head, but Drew mumbled, "Credit."

"Credit? He owed you money?"

"Shut up, Drew," Hoppy said.

"What difference does it make?" said Drew. "He's dead. We'll never get it back now."

He stopped walking and turned to Rory.

"He brought his fancy car in for a full-out overhaul. We left him the keys like we do for our best customers, so he could get the car after we closed. He never paid us."

"Nothing?"

"Not a dime," said Drew. "Told us that night he'd make it good when we all got back. But then he didn't get back."

"Look," said Hoppy. "I know it sounds bad. But if I were you, I'd have a word with Mark Jacob. He talked to the guy at the telescope, yes, but I heard him talking earlier to someone at the boat. I couldn't hear the words, but it was a man's voice so it couldn't be Karen."

The group took Detective Gallardo and Sergeant
Maura around the outside of the house,
showing them where Mark Jacob's telescope had
been set up, where everyone was standing, and
the location where they saw the victim. Maura
was taking careful notes.

"The plants are gorgeous," said Rosie. She
was standing with Arnold and Lou near the
water pump, gazing up at the building. It looked
Victorian, with a tall turret and pointed gables.
Ivy crawled up the walls and a rambling pale
pink rose covered the arbor over the front door.

"Just look at that jasmine," agreed Arnold,
pointing at a vine snaking up the downspout
from the second story, covering it with tiny

white five-pointed flowers. There was yellow crime tape all around it.

"That's not jasmine; it's trachelospermum," said Rosie. Lou managed to hide his laughter.

"Which one of them did it?" said Lou.

"I don't know," said Rosie. "The problem is they could all be lying."

"What do you mean?" asked Arnold.

"I think each one of them encountered Thomas Zinn apart from the others that night. The last one who did must have killed him."

They stood in silence for a moment, then Rosie tilted her head.

"Did you think it odd that Doctor Jacob didn't set up the telescope last night? He brought it all the way here."

"That's right," said Lou. "Probably distracted by the murder investigation."

"Arnold," she said. "That crime tape is where you think Thomas Zinn was strangled?"

"Yes, that's the area," he said, nodding toward the vine.

"Oh, geez," said Rosie. "I know who did it."

Lou was grumbling again. "Isn't it too Hercules Poirot to have everyone here in the dock house to hear Rosie's solution?"

"I don't have a problem with it," answered Rory. "Keeps everyone where I can see them." He nodded to Sergeant Maura, who was standing in the doorway.

But instead of speaking, Rosie sat down on the edge of the cot and prepared to listen to Detective Rory Gallardo explain his theory. It had not escaped her notice that Sergeant Maura was blocking the only exit and that his handcuffs were hanging off the front of his belt rather than the back.

"Before we head back to San Benno," Rory began, "I'd like to share with you what we know about Thomas Zinn, the man you saw here on the island. The man who was killed."

Arnold and Lou were seated in chairs, Karen was on the floor with her paperback turned over on her knee, the brothers were standing in the corner, and Mark Jacob was next to the window.

"We know that the victim ripped off Drew and Hoppy over getting his car repaired, and that there was an altercation here on the island. That happened late at night, apparently, after you all had seen him at the telescope. And you brothers together would have no trouble subduing him."

"But we didn't kill him," said Hoppy.

"No, you didn't. We also know Karen Aguilar had some kind of conversation with a man at the boat earlier that day. But the big news is this: the victim, Thomas Zinn, owned this island and the house, and from Ron Voss's papers we know he had no intention of selling. I'm sure that made all of you unhappy."

A pin could drop, thought Rosie, it was so quiet. The waves could be heard lapping at the dock.

"But it's Mark Jacob who killed him," Rory announced.

"What?" Jacob jumped. "Why on earth would I do that? I barely knew the man."

"Not true," said Rosie. "I did a bit of research before we came. You love astronomy, Dr. Jacob. You've been studying it for years. And yet I noticed you didn't set up your telescope last night. Why was that?"

"Not in the mood," said Jacob.

"You're actually fairly well known. *Science* magazine even accepted one of your articles, and it had a little bio at the bottom. You worked under a Dr. Thomas Zinn at CalTech, the same guy who just published an article about A13-742. And is now dead because of it."

"What the hell is A13-742?" said Lou.

"It's a cepheid variable," said Rosie.

Lou gave her a look.

"A star," she said, removing a sprig with white flowers from her pocket. "I believe you like to garden, Doctor Jacob?"

His eyes were wary but he nodded.

"You killed him near the trachelospermum." She twirled the sprig in her fingers. "It's a vine commonly known as Star Jasmine. You were being symbolic. Zinn stole your star."

Mark Jacob's body stiffened. But there were tears on his cheeks.

"I discovered her, my beautiful star. Here on the island, alone on that hill. She was mine."

He looked miserable. Karen sniffed. The brothers looked at the floor.

"It's not easy sneaking a dead body back across the channel," said Rory softly. "Zinn would need to be carried back to his own boat, which Sergeant Maura discovered up the beach. The murderer would need help."

There was silence. The brothers and Karen glanced at each other. Arnold's eyes opened so wide they looked like sand dollars.

"Good heavens, they're accessories," Arnold sputtered.

"I'm afraid so," said Rory, as Diego Maura cuffed Mark Jacob. "I hope you'll understand why we'll need to secure you all for the trip back."

"I don't know how you do it, Rosie-me-darling." Lou was comfortably ensconced on Rosie's sofa with the orange cat in his lap. "I'll write the story first thing in the morning."

"It must be a terrible thing," Rosie said as she brought in two cups of tea. "To have something like that taken from you."

"But he had very good friends," Lou said. "Crazy friends, but good ones. That's gotta be important."

"Oh it is," said Rosie, thinking she should plant some Star Jasmine. "Can't do much without good friends."

Want more of Rosie and Lou? Read their first murder-solving adventure in Bummer at Luna Beach. *For more on Lisa's books, visit https://grousablebooks.com.*